W9-DGY-267

There are Abbotts and there are Abbotts. These Abbotts are rabbits. The rabbit Abbotts make the designs on Easter eggs.

Their son Orson thought he wanted to be an artist, too. He was going to try to help with the eggs next Easter.

Father Abbott looked at the picture Orson had made to show what he could do.

"Well," he said to Mother Abbott, "it's not bad for five minutes' work. But look at him out there—he's forgotten all about it."

"Remember, he's still a youngster and needs to play," said Mother Abbott.

"That's what I mean. He may not be much help."

The Abbotts ordered one hundred dozen eggs to be delivered in January.

"We should be back from our vacation by then," Father Abbott said. "And we will have plenty of time to finish painting the eggs by Easter."

"It is already October," Mother Abbott said. "We should leave soon if we want to get south before the cold weather comes."

"First, the car needs painting," said Father Abbott.

"Not the whole thing," Orson said. "Just the rusty parts. I'll do it." Then he saw the grin on his father's face and said, "Well, at least I'll help. Let's make the car and trailer look like Easter eggs."

"Great idea!" said Father Abbott.

They worked together covering the rusty spots with their special designs.

Then off the Abbotts went on their trip. They took along everything they would need for camping, and their paints and brushes too, just in case.

"Wow!" Orson said after a while. "People really like the way we painted the car. Everybody's looking! Dad, how do you make purple? Red and blue together?"

"Right!" said Father Abbott. "Fasten your seat belt."

The Abbotts drove south, and farther south, looking for nice weather and a good place to set up camp.

At last they reached the warm sea. Orson had never seen so much water.

They set up camp and spent long days on the beach.

Orson wore his red life belt. He galloped in the sand and splashed in the sea.

Mother and Father Abbott drew portraits of everyone who wanted to pay for them.

When the Abbotts had had enough of that, they went traveling again, just poking around. People were always offering them jobs because of the beautiful designs on the car and trailer.

They even decorated the outside of an entire house. Orson did all of the high parts. It was easy for him to keep his balance on the slanting roof, and he liked looking down and out over the trees.

A plane advertising the county fair buzzed the house. The pilot landed and came to get a closer look.

Well, naturally, he wanted his plane decorated.

"Oh, wow!" Orson yelled.

"Hmm," Father Abbott said. "Shouldn't the decorations be on the bottom? People look *up* at a plane."

"Top and bottom," the pilot said. "I do aerobatics."

"What's that?" Orson asked.

"I make the plane tumble over and over in the sky."

Orson shivered with delight.

He worked hard decorating the plane. Maybe the pilot would take him for a ride in the sky if he liked the designs.

He did!

Orson and the pilot circled over the Abbotts' camp.

"Orson has really changed," Father Abbott said. "Keeping his mind on his work until it's finished—he's growing up fast."

"It helps when people notice what you do and enjoy it," Mother Abbott said.

"It seems to work that way. When we were in town shopping this afternoon we were asked if we would decorate the bridge over the river. Orson spoke right up and said we'd be glad to. And on the way home he asked me if he could do it all by himself!"

"Fine," said Mother Abbott. "We'll have fun just watching for a change."

*Everybody* came to watch. Orson loved it. He was busy for a long time, but he never got tired.

It was January when he finished, and the Abbotts had to hurry home and start painting the Easter eggs.

Would Orson be able to settle down and work in the studio after all that had happened? Would he be interested in painting Easter eggs?

"One hundred dozen," Father Abbott said to himself. "That's twelve hundred eggs. Six hundred apiece, if we have to do them all without Orson's help."

The eggs were there when the Abbotts got home. Goose eggs, duck eggs, chicken eggs—and OSTRICH eggs, too.

It was the ostrich eggs that got Orson interested.

He tried one—and another and another. Soon he was working as hard as he had worked on the bridge.

He was having a wonderful time because . . .

. . . . he had invented comic Easter eggs! People wanted to buy them faster than he could paint them.

His parents finally had to start helping *him* to keep up with the orders.

Father Abbott was forever on the telephone, ordering more eggs or taking new orders.

Orson was laughing. "Whoever finds *this* is going to get a shock!" he shouted.

Easter came at last. All of the orders had been filled and shipped out. The only eggs left were for the Abbotts' annual Easter Egg Hunt. The little rabbits of the neighborhood were eager and waiting.

The Abbotts, all three of them, hid the eggs the night before, by flashlight.

The next morning Mother and Father Abbott were tired and sleepy. But not Orson. He was up and out. He climbed into a tree where he could watch the little ones hunt the eggs.

His parents couldn't resist. They had to get up and look out the window *once*.

"Well!" was all Father Abbott could say, and Mother Abbott smiled sleepily.

During the day the spring weather grew warm. Mother and Father Abbott were taking it easy outdoors.

"Where's Orson?" Mother Abbott wondered.

"He was working on something in the studio a while ago," Father Abbott said, "but no telling where he might be now."

"Orson Abbott, the Easter Egg artist," Mother Abbott said fondly.

"Yes," Father Abbott said, "and car artist and house artist, and airplane and bridge!"

"Don't look now," said Mother Abbott, "but *flagpole,* too!"